Franklin's New Friend

Franklin

Franklin is a trademark of Kids Can Press Ltd.

Text © 1997 Contextx Inc.
Illustrations © 1997 Brenda Clark Illustrator Inc.

Interior illustrations prepared with the assistance of
Muriel Hughes Wood.

Kids Can Press acknowledges the financial support of the Ontario Arts
Council, the Canada Council for the Arts and the Government of
Canada, through the CBF, for our publishing activity.

Published in Canada by
Kids Can Press Ltd.
25 Dockside Drive
Toronto, ON M5A 0B5

Published in the U.S. by
Kids Can Press Ltd.
2250 Military Road
Tonawanda, NY 14150

www.kidscanpress.com

The hardcover edition of this book is smyth sewn casebound.
The paperback edition of this book is limp sewn with a drawn-on cover.
Manufactured in Buji, Shenzhen, China, in 5/2014 by WKT Company

CM 97 0 9 8 7 6 5 4
CDN PA 97 0 9
CMC PA 14 0 9 8 7 6 5 4 3 2 1

Library and Archives Canada Cataloguing in Publication

Bourgeois, Paulette
   Franklin's new friend / Paulette Bourgeois ; illustrated by
Brenda Clark.

For ages 3–8.
(A classic Franklin story)
ISBN 978-1-55453-773-0

   1. Franklin (Fictitious character : Bourgeois) — Juvenile fiction.
I. Clark, Brenda II. Title.

PS8553.O85477F87 2011   jC813'.54   C2011-901339-8

Kids Can Press is a lorus™ Entertainment company

Franklin's New Friend

Written by Paulette Bourgeois
Illustrated by Brenda Clark

Kids Can Press

FRANKLIN had always lived in the same house in the same town. He had grown up with his friends, and each one had a special place in Franklin's life.

When Franklin wanted to play hide and seek, he called Fox. If Franklin needed a best friend, he called Bear.

Franklin never thought about making friends until a new family moved in down the lane.

Franklin was curious about the newcomers.
He rubbed his eyes as the movers unloaded
the furniture. The beds were made for giants,
and the lamps were as tall as trees.
When Franklin finally saw the family, he
was speechless.

Franklin had never met a moose before. He had heard about moose. He had seen pictures of moose. But he had never actually known one. They were huge. Even the smallest moose was big.

Franklin was so scared that he raced home.

"A moose family moved in!"

"That's nice," said Franklin's mother. "Maybe you'll make a new friend."

Franklin shook his head. "I don't think so."

"I expect you to be nice when you meet someone new," warned his mother.

Franklin scowled.

The next morning, there was a moose in Franklin's classroom.

"Please give a warm welcome to your new classmate," said Mr. Owl.

"Hello, Moose," said the class in unison.
Moose mumbled hello and looked at his feet.
"He doesn't look very friendly," whispered Beaver.

Mr. Owl told the class that Moose had come from a different place, far away.

"Franklin," said Mr. Owl, "I'd like you to be a buddy for Moose."

Franklin tried to smile but he was scared. Moose was so big!

Moose didn't say a word all morning.

At recess, Franklin ran outside with his friends, leaving Moose behind. But Mr. Owl reminded Franklin that he was Moose's buddy.

"Do you want to play?" asked Franklin.

Moose shook his head back and forth.

Franklin was relieved.

During recess, Moose stood alone as Franklin and his friends played soccer.

Fox kicked the ball too hard, and it flew into a tree.

"Now we'll have to get Mr. Owl," groaned Bear.

"I've got it!" cried Moose. He knocked the ball out of the tree and sent it flying to Franklin.

"That was good," said Fox.

"I guess," shrugged Franklin.

Back in the classroom, Mr. Owl asked Franklin and Moose to make a poster for the bake sale.

"I don't need any help," said Franklin.

Mr. Owl talked to Franklin alone. "Try to imagine how Moose feels. He's new and he has no friends here. He's probably scared."

"Moose can't be scared," said Franklin. "He's so big."

Mr. Owl looked at Franklin. "Big or little, we all get scared."

Franklin thought about that.

Franklin got the paints and the paper.
"Do you want to help me, Moose?"
"Oh, yes," said Moose. "I love to draw."
They sat side by side and planned the poster together.
Franklin realized that Moose didn't seem as big when he was sitting.

After much work, the poster was perfect. They both thought so.

At library time, Franklin taught Moose how to borrow books.

Moose showed Franklin how to cut a
perfect circle.
    They both liked to build structures.
    Franklin and Moose had a lot in common.

At lunch, Franklin made sure that Bear and his other friends got to know his new buddy. They liked Moose. Besides, he was a very good soccer player.

When Franklin got home from school, he was happy.

"Guess what?" he told his mother. "I have a new friend."

"So you met Moose?" asked his mother. "What's he like?"

"Moose is big," said Franklin. "But he's not mean or scary."

"Good," said his mother. "Would you like to take some of these cookies to him?"

Franklin went to Moose's house.
They ate all the cookies together.
"I'm glad you were my buddy," said
Moose. "I was worried that nobody would
play with me."
"Really?" said Franklin. He could barely
remember being afraid of Moose.

From then on, Franklin and Moose
played together all the time. Now Franklin's
new friend was a special friend.